What is a Bird?

by Jenifer W. Day
illustrated by Tony Chen

A GOLDEN BOOK · NEW YORK
Western Publishing Company, Inc., Racine, Wisconsin 53404

This is a robin.
A robin is a bird.
A robin can sing.
A robin is a songbird.

Songbirds have feathers.
Songbirds lay eggs.
Songbirds have wings.
Songbirds can fly.

Rose-breasted
Grosbeak

Waxwing

Cardinal

Goldfinch

Painted
Bunting

There are many kinds of songbirds.

Flicker

Chickadee

Tanager

Hoopoo

Cuckoo

Finch

Blue Jay

This is a macaw.
A macaw is a bird.
A macaw is a tropical bird.
Tropical birds live in forests
    where the climate is warm.

Bird of Paradise

Parakeet

Toucan

Cock-of-the-Rock

Motmot

There are many kinds of tropical birds.

This is an owl.
An owl is a bird.
Owls sleep in the day
  and feed at night.
They eat mice
  and other small animals.

Great Horned Owl

Owls have feathers.
Owls lay eggs.
Owls have wings.
Owls can fly.

Screech
Owl

Snowy Owl

Barn
Owl

Spectacled
Owl

There are many kinds of owls.

Bald Eagle

This is an eagle.
An eagle is a bird of prey.
Birds of prey feed on other animals.
They have strong sharp beaks
    and long sharp claws.

Birds of prey have feathers.
Birds of prey lay eggs.
Birds of prey have very strong wings
and can fly very high.

Sparrow Hawk

Kite

Harris
Hawk

Osprey

There are many birds of prey.

This is a turkey.
A turkey is a bird.
A turkey is a land bird.
Land birds scratch for their food,
    and usually build their nests
    on the ground.

Land birds have feathers.
Land birds lay eggs.
Land birds have wings.
Land birds can fly—but not very high.

There are many kinds of land birds.

Rooster

Quail

Golden
Pheasant

Peacock

These birds are ducks.
Ducks are waterfowl.
Waterfowl are birds
    that live near ponds
    and marshes.
They feed mainly on water plants.
They have long necks, short legs,
    and webbed feet.

Black Duck

Mallard Duck

Waterfowl have feathers.
Waterfowl lay eggs.
Waterfowl have wings.
Waterfowl can fly—far, far away.
They can also swim.

There are many kinds of waterfowl.

Mute Swan

Canada Goose

Mandarin Duck

White Stork

This is a stork.
A stork is a bird.
A stork is a wading bird
    with long legs
    and a long neck.
Wading birds find their food
    in the water.
They eat fish, snakes, insects,
    and other small animals.

Wading birds have feathers.
Wading birds lay eggs.
Wading birds have wings.
Wading birds can fly.

There are many kinds
of wading birds.

Saddle-bill Stork

Flamingo

Spoonbill

Night
Heron

Great
Blue Heron

This is a pelican.
A pelican is a bird
that lives near
or on the water.
Pelicans swim and dive
and feed on fish.

Brown Pelican

Frigatebird

Herring Gull

Tern

Cormorant

Puffin

There are many fish-eating birds
that swim and dive
and live near the sea.

This is an ostrich.
An ostrich is a bird.
An ostrich is the largest bird alive.
An ostrich has a long neck and long legs
   and can run very fast.

An ostrich has feathers.
An ostrich lays eggs.
An ostrich has wings
   but it cannot fly.
An ostrich is a flightless bird.

Penguins are flightless birds.
Penguins have feathers.
Penguins lay eggs.
But penguins use
    their wings to swim
    in the cold icy water.

Emperor Penguin

King Penguin

Jackass Penguin

Rockhopper Penguin

There are many kinds of birds.
There are many sizes of birds.
There are many colors of birds.
There are land birds
    and water birds.
There are big birds
    and little birds.

There are red birds,
    blue birds,
    green birds,
    yellow birds,
    and even multicolored birds.

But what is a bird?

Kingfisher

Screamer

Merganser

Grebe

Yellowthroat

Flycatcher

Red Bishop

Purple Gallinule

Bluebird

Green Magpie

Purple-backed
Wren

Hornbill

Scarlet Ibis

Cassowary

A bird is an animal
that has feathers,
and lays eggs,
and has wings.
Most birds can fly.

The hummingbird
is the smallest bird of all.